To the fears I've embraced — F.P.

To the wolf — A.S.

This edition published by Kids Can Press in 2023

Originally published in 2022 in Spain by AKIARA books, SLU, under the title *Per què tenim por?*
Published by agreement with AKIARA books, SLU, through the VeroK Agency, Barcelona, Spain.

Text © 2022 Fran Pintadera
Illustrations © 2022 Ana Sender
English translation by Mihaila Petricic
English translation © 2023 Kids Can Press

Published in Canada and the U.S. by Kids Can Press Ltd.
25 Dockside Drive, Toronto, ON M5A 0B5

Kids Can Press is a Corus Entertainment Inc. company

www.kidscanpress.com

English edition edited by Katie Scott

Printed and bound in Shenzhen, China,
in 10/2022 by C & C Offset

CM 23 0 9 8 7 6 5 4 3 2 1

FSC
www.fsc.org
MIX
Paper | Supporting
responsible forestry
FSC® C008047

Library and Archives Canada Cataloguing in Publication

Title: Why are we afraid? / written by Fran Pintadera ; illustrated by Ana Sender.
Other titles: Per què tenim por? English
Names: Pintadera, Fran, 1982– author. | Sender, Ana, 1978– illustrator.
Description: Translation of: Per què tenim por? | Translated from the Catalan.
Identifiers: Canadiana 20220267804 | ISBN 9781525311291 (hardcover)
Classification: LCC PZ7.1.P56 Wha 2023 | DDC j863/.7 — dc23

Kids Can Press gratefully acknowledges that the land on which our office is located is the traditional territory of many nations, including the Mississaugas of the Credit, the Anishnabeg, the Chippewa, the Haudenosaunee and the Wendat peoples, and is now home to many diverse First Nations, Inuit and Métis peoples.

We thank the Government of Ontario, through Ontario Creates for supporting our publishing activity.

WHY ARE WE AFRAID?

Written by Fran Pintadera
Illustrated by Ana Sender

Kids Can Press

After the clap of thunder, the house went dark.

Max's father lit a large red candle and set it on the table.

Max watched the flame dance for a few minutes. Then he asked,

"Dad, have you ever been afraid?"

Max's father closed his eyes to gather his thoughts.

"Yes, Max, I have," he said at last. "We're all afraid sometimes. It doesn't matter if our fears are small or imaginary. They can **flood the room** in an instant.

"Some people are afraid of the **unknown**.
They don't want to lose their way in the maze.

"Others are afraid to face the shadows.
They feel it's too hard.

"Sometimes we're afraid of loud **words** and roaring **blows**. They can make us tremble like leaves in the wind.

"We can be afraid of feeling **lonely** or of being **alone**. People need people. Being around others can warm us like a fire.

"Sometimes we're afraid because the **real monsters** aren't under the bed after all.

"We're afraid of **losing what we love**, forgetting that the important things were never meant to be owned.

"Often we're afraid of freedom,

strange as it seems.

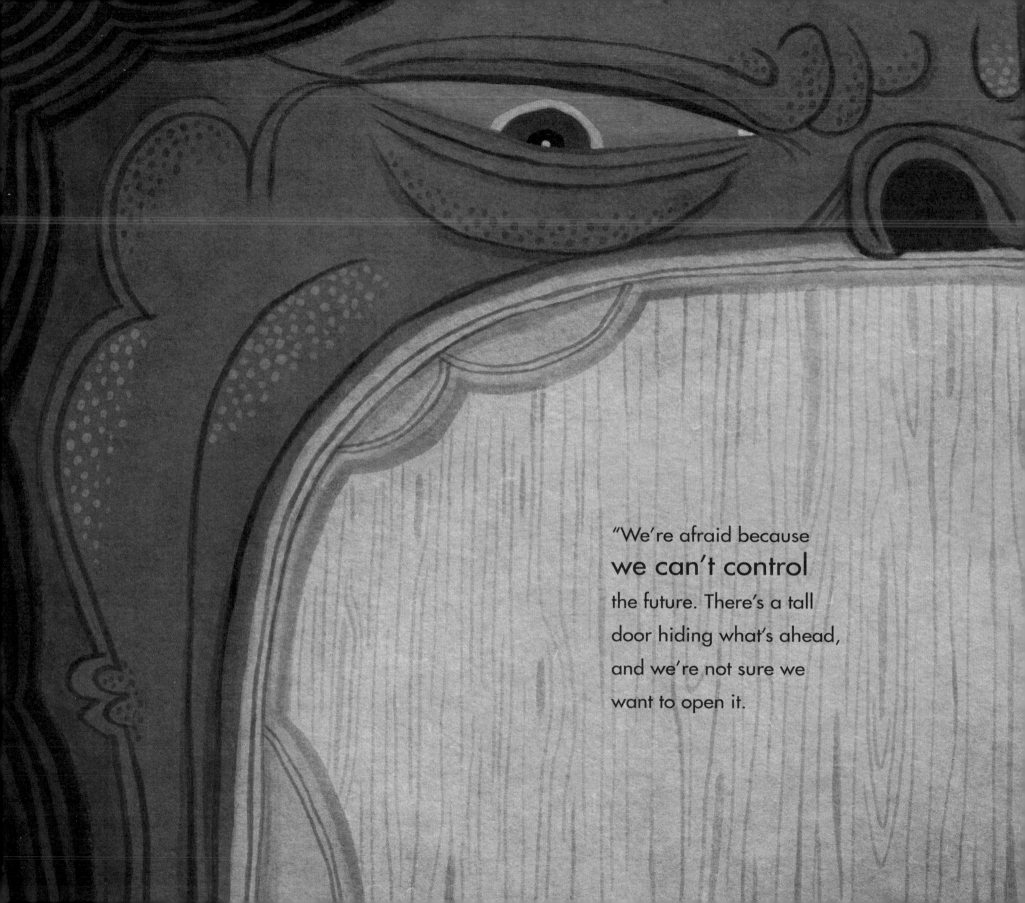

"We're afraid because **we can't control** the future. There's a tall door hiding what's ahead, and we're not sure we want to open it.

"We're afraid of
falling short,

of free-falling

and of fading away.

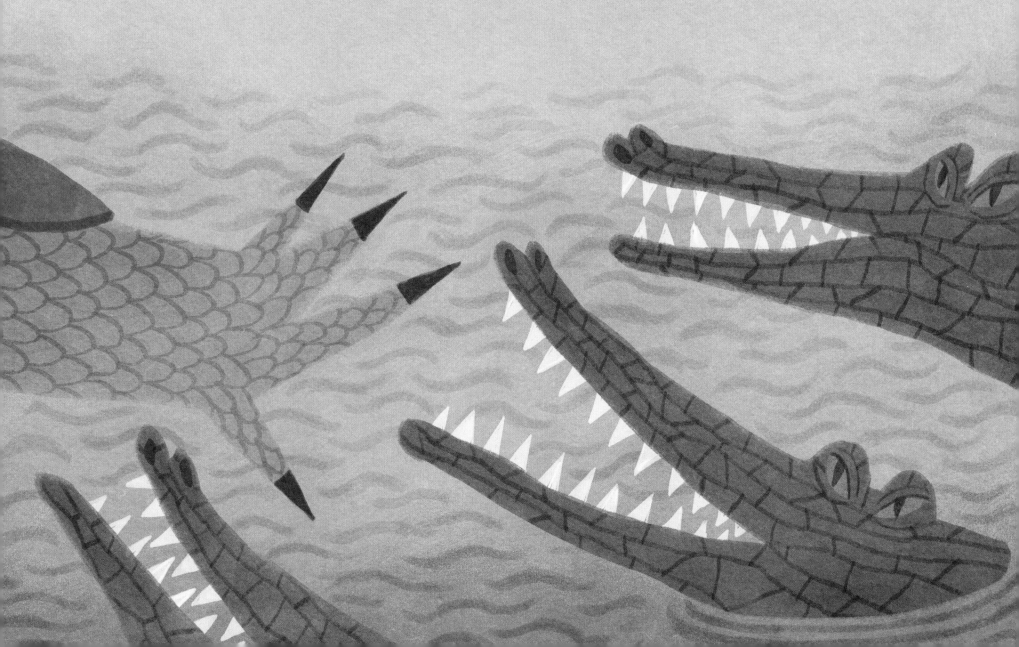

"Some people hide behind heavy armor to mask their fears. They're afraid their **armor will crack open** and expose them. But they don't usually tell you that.

"Some of our fears feel so powerful that they stop us in our tracks. Like a guiding lighthouse, they can warn us of the danger ahead.

Either way, Max, **we always keep going.**"

Outside, the streetlights came on — the power was back. Max's father went to turn on the light switch, but Max stopped him.

"Dad, can we let the candle burn a bit longer? It's the perfect night for **telling stories**."

Max's father smiled and sat down beside him.

"Sure. What would you like to hear?"

Max hesitated for a moment.

Finally, he asked,

"Do you know any scary stories?"

SHINING A LIGHT ON FEAR

The original fear

Fear is one of our basic emotions. It's been around as long as we have. Chimpanzees, our distant relatives, are scared of many of the same things we are. Imagine you went back in time and met the first people on Earth. How do you think they felt in the wild, knowing they could be eaten by animals? Imagine their bodies tensing up as they tuned in to every twig snap. That's our primal — or original — fear talking. It's the first fear we ever had: the fear of disappearing. And it helped us build our survival instincts to stay safe from danger.

After all this time, we still have the same fear. It might sound strange, but growing up, moving and starting something new are all ways of disappearing. Even though we don't literally go "poof!" and vanish, some things go away with time: our identities, our opinions, our masks, our roles in the world and the stories we tell ourselves. And that can be scary.

The types of fear

There are two types of fear: innate and learned. Innate fears are the ones we're born with. They travel with us through life. They've existed for hundreds of generations and will continue to exist for hundreds more. Learned fears, on the other hand, are fears we learn along the way, either from our personal experience or because we inherit them from someone. However they got into our suitcase, they become our compass. Sometimes our fears are justified and get us moving, like when our survival instincts kick in. Other times, we have less typical fears that can get out of hand. These are sometimes called irrational fears. And then there are some downright bizarre fears — like being scared of tomatoes!

The lessons behind our fears

Generally, our fears let us know when there's something about ourselves to explore. They're an opportunity to reach into the deepest places within ourselves. In stories from long ago and in books and movies today, the hero encounters beasts, monsters, ogres and dragons. These creatures symbolize our fears — the hurdles that stand in the way of our desires. When the hero conquers their fears, that's when they've won. They emerge victorious not because they've vanquished a villain, but because they've become a new, wiser version of themselves. When we overcome our fears and can look them square in the eye, we find out what we're made of.

The masks of fear

Fear is associated with darkness — maybe because it prefers to stay hidden. If we shine a light on it and say, "Aha! Gotcha!" it'll stop in its tracks. And once it's out in the open, we can do away with it more easily. But as long as it insists on going unnoticed, it can take on many masks, disguising itself as caution, protection or shame. Sometimes it even tries to be our friend. Fears that we inherit from others — the ones we learn along the way — can seem so unlike us at first. But they insist on traveling with us so much and so often that they end up driving us. That's why it's important to recognize what our fears are trying to do. Are they trying to keep us safe or prevent us from following our dreams? Fear can protect us and get us moving, but it can also paralyze us. When that happens, we can talk to it and cut through its mask until it's exposed. All that's left to do then is embrace it.

The appeal of fear

Scary as it is, we like fear. Or at least some kinds of fear. We like watching scary movies, exploring abandoned houses and listening to hair-raising stories by the fire. You could say we like playing with fear.

And why shouldn't we? As one of our basic emotions, it's part of who we are, so it's normal that we want to explore it. Fear needs to be expressed, and when words fall short, the body takes over: the hair on our arms and the backs of our necks stands up, our hearts start beating faster and our bodies tense up, waiting for the jump scare. Exploring and expressing our fears can make us feel alive, just like the first people on the planet.

Activities

1. Sometimes our sense of fear doesn't turn on when it should. In the story, after the streetlights go out, Max's father compares fear to a lighthouse. What if the lighthouse didn't light up when it should? Or if the light always stayed on? Think of a time when you've been afraid. Did your sense of fear ever turn off when you needed it most? What about the other way around? Has your fear shone a light on something you didn't need to be afraid of?

2. Take a moment to explore and express your fears. What are your biggest fears? Write down the words that describe how your fears look, sound or feel. Then draw what those fears look like to you.